For Adam
KH

For Sam, Tom, Jo and
Lucy with love
HC

Text copyright © 1988 by Katharine Holabird
Illustrations copyright © 1988 by Helen Craig

Published in the United States by Clarkson N. Potter, Inc., 225 Park Avenue South, New York, New York 10003, and represented in Canada by the Canadian MANDA Group

Published in Great Britain by Aurum Books for Children, 33 Museum Street, London WC1A 1LD

CLARKSON N. POTTER, POTTER, and colophon are trademarks of Clarkson N. Potter, Inc.

Manufactured in Italy

Library of Congress Cataloguing-in-Publication Data
Holabird, Katharine.
  Alexander and the dragon/illustrations by Helen Craig: story by
Katharine Holabird.
    p.   cm.
  Summary: A very small boy is afraid of the dark, especially when
the shadow under his bed becomes a fierce dragon. He soon learns,
however, that even dragons have their gentle side.
  ISBN: 0–517–56996–5
  [1. Dragons—Fiction.   2. Night—Fiction.   3. Fear—Fiction.]
I. Craig, Helen, 111.   II. Title.
PZ7.H689A1 1988
[E]—dc19   88–5825
                                                                         CIP
                                                                          AC

10 9 8 7 6 5 4 3 2 1

First Edition

Alexander
and the Dragon

Story by Katharine Holabird Illustrations by Helen Craig

Clarkson N. Potter, Inc./Publishers NEW YORK
DISTRIBUTED BY CROWN PUBLISHERS, INC.

Alexander was quite small, but he was very, very brave.
He wasn't afraid of dogs or thunderstorms; he liked
riding on roller coasters and swimming underwater.
The only thing that really frightened Alexander was the dark.

He always hated to be alone in his room at nighttime.
His mother left his night-light on and read him stories
to cheer him up but as soon as she tucked him in
and went downstairs, Alexander began to imagine
all sorts of awful things.

He imagined that his door
was a mean giant,
and that his curtains
were two ugly witches,
and that his chest of drawers
was a fat old bear.

Then he would be very brave and leap out of his
bed and run all the way downstairs to his mother.
She would take Alexander up again and say,
"Those are only shadows, darling. Don't be afraid."

But as soon as his mother had left the room,
Alexander would hide under the covers and
put a pillow over his head.

One night at bedtime Alexander noticed a dark
shadow sitting right under his bed.

"I don't like that shadow," he said to his mother.

"There's nothing there. Beds always have shadows and they can't hurt you. Now try to go to sleep," she said as she kissed him goodnight.

But when she was gone, Alexander was sure there was a dragon under his bed. He was so scared that he didn't dare move, and it took him a long time to fall asleep.

At breakfast the next morning, Alexander said, "There is a dragon under my bed so I can't sleep in my room anymore."

"Hmmm," said Alexander's father. "There are only two things you can do with a dragon. You've either got to scare it off or make friends with it."

And then Alexander's father went off to work.

That afternoon Alexander put on his special helmet and shield and found his shining red sword at the bottom of his toy box. He tiptoed up to his room, his heart beating loudly in his chest. Whatever happened, he had decided to be strong and brave.

"DRAGON!" shouted Alexander loudly. "Come out of my room or I'll bash you!"

The dragon growled and its shadow lengthened
into a great green tail that slid from under the bed.

Alexander swung his red sword over his head
and bashed the bedpost until the dragon
snarled and flashed its yellow teeth.

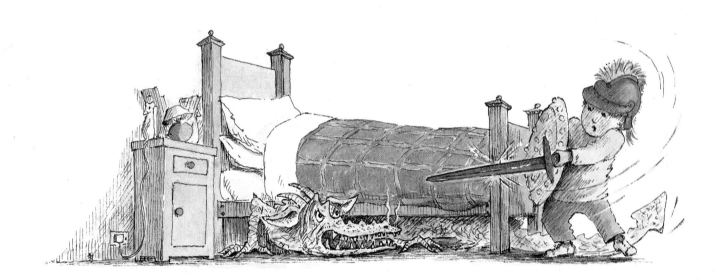

Again and again Alexander
    charged at the hiding dragon,
        and finally managed to whack it hard on the nose.

"Ooh!" cried the dragon. "That hurts!"

Alexander stopped and peered under the bed.
The dragon's face was sad and frightened,
and he wasn't snarling at all.

"Come out from under my bed, please,"
said Alexander as he put down his sword.
"I promise I won't hurt you."

The dragon slowly crawled out and laid its head on Alexander's lap. "I didn't know that dragons could talk," said Alexander, scratching the dragon's ear.

"I didn't know that little boys could be so polite," said the dragon.

"At first I thought you were a shadow," Alexander told the dragon.

"Most dragons these days look like shadows when you first see them," explained the dragon, "and most people never can tell the difference."

"Will you stay and play with me?" asked Alexander.

So the dragon stayed in Alexander's room.
Sometimes it hid in the corner or under
the bed and looked just like a shadow.
Only when Alexander was alone did the
dragon come out and play with him.

"I made friends with the dragon under my bed and it's not scary at all," Alexander told his parents that evening.

"I thought he might be a friendly one," said Alexander's father.

"I'm very proud of you, Alexander," his mother said.

"The good thing is," added Alexander, "I'm not afraid of shadows anymore and I don't even need a night-light."

So after that,
Alexander slept
in the dark
and the friendly
dragon kept him
company.